Harold Shows O...
Reading Book

Illustrated by Niall Harding
Written by Brenda Apsley

Thomas the Tank Engine & Friends

A BRITT ALLCROFT COMPANY PRODUCTION

Based on The Railway Series by The Rev W Awdry

© Gullane (Thomas) LLC 2003

Published in Great Britain in 2003 by Egmont Books Limited, 239 Kensington High Street, London, W8 6SA
Printed in China   ISBN 0 7498 5766 8

1 3 5 7 9 10 8 6 4 2

This pre-reading programme ...

is designed to encourage an early confidence in reading.
It features the 45 frequent-use words as set out in the
National Curriculum, plus key vocabulary from the
Thomas Learning programme.

Listening to stories provides a very strong motivation for children to make the effort
to learn to read themselves. Thomas and friends are well-loved characters.
Children need exciting characters in stories so they will enjoy learning to read.

There is lots of repetition of key words and phrases. This encourages recognition of
words and the link between their sounds and shapes. Your child will also begin to
predict what is coming next, thus connecting written and spoken words, enabling
them to 'read'.

To get the most out of the Look and Say books:

· read the stories several times with your child on different occasions;

· read the speech in a lively, animated style and point to the words;

· encourage your child to read aloud the words he/she has learned.

Other activities to enjoy

· **Match the pictures**

Children will scan the page from left to right in preparation for reading and writing.

· **Find the pictures**

Children will learn to observe small details in this activity.

· **Spot the difference**

Children will compare two pictures - a skill used in reading when distinguishing letter shapes and words.

Harold was a big helicopter.

Harold said he was better than
the engines.

"I can fly," Harold said to Thomas.

"You can only go on rails."

"Look at me," said Harold.

"I can go up and down,"
said Harold.

"Show me," said Thomas.
"Go up and down."

Harold went up and down.

"I can go round and round,"
said Harold.

"Show me," said Thomas.
"Go round and round."

Harold went round and round,
and up and down.

It made Harold dizzy.

Harold went from side to side.

It made Harold very dizzy.

"You can't fly now!" said Thomas.

"But I can go! Look at me!"

Draw a line between the pictures that are the same.

Point to these things in the picture.

Spot the difference!

Point to 5 differences between
these two pictures.

Thomas Reading

(age 4-6)

Develop your child's reading confidence with these six reading books, companion activity books and flash cards.

Thomas Maths

(age 4-6)

Introduce your child to early maths skills with these six maths story books, companion activity books and flash cards.